Prairie Meeting

by Linda Baxter

Cover Illustration: Doug Knutson
Inside Illustration: Jenny Heath

For the grandfather I never knew.

L.B.

About the Author

Linda Baxter was born in Cheyenne, Wyoming, and traveled with her military family, finally settling in Tempe, Arizona. She graduated with a degree in elementary education from Arizona State University. Linda taught elementary grades in Phoenix, Arizona, and Catshill, Bromsgrove, England.

She lives with her husband, Dave, and three children in Monte Sereno, California.

Text © 1998 by Perfection Learning® Corporation.

All rights reserved. No part of this book may be used or reproduced in any manner whatsoever without written permission from the publisher.

Printed in the United States of America. For information, contact Perfection Learning® Corporation, 1000 North Second Avenue P.O. Box 500, Logan, Iowa 51546–1099.

Paperback ISBN 0-7891-2160-3

Cover Craft® ISBN 0-7807-6787-x

Contents

1

Auf Wiedersehen!

Paul lugged the huge bag out of the carriage and took his first look at the ship. Its white bow stood high in the water, towering over him.

His father helped his mother down from the hired coach. There were already tears in her eyes. Paul hoped she wouldn't cry now. Then how would he keep from crying?

Paul pushed his strong chin forward and steeled himself. He tried to smooth down the blond hair that curled over his brow. Then he put on his cap. His light blue eyes studied the scene around him.

The dock was filled with people saying good-bye. They were surrounded by odd-shaped bundles and large trunks. Some bundles were new and shiny, bound with belts. Others showed signs of many trips. A few were nothing more than a cloth sack.

Far above their heads, the first-class travelers boarded on a wide, covered gangplank. Black-coated servants lifted their luggage aboard.

Paul had brought what he could carry in a strong leather bag. Uncle Olaf had warned in a letter not to bring more than he could handle alone.

Paul's mother had made him a new suit of clothes. She had sewn extra material into the seams and hems. But the dull, brown suit was a little lumpy in places.

"You're still growing, Paul. You will need the room," Mama had said when Paul had tried the suit on last night. "I made the suit of good strong fabric. It will last you a long time." Paul knew she had spent many hours at the treadle sewing machine.

Paul's father had already bought the ticket. He handed it to Paul.

Suddenly, Paul could hardly breathe. In just a little while, he would get on this ship and sail away. All the way to America! Up to this very moment, the trip across the sea had seemed a dream. It was some other boy who was going to America. America!

Then Paul looked down at his little sister Elisabete. Paul suddenly felt very lonely. Elisabete's pudgy little arms reached up to him, asking him to lift her.

Paul dropped his bag and took Elisabete in his arms. He held her so tight that she squirmed and gave a pouting look, with her lower lip stuck out.

"Don't worry, my little Itty," whispered Paul. "Pauli will be back to get you someday. I will write to you. And when you learn, you can write to me."

"Can I paint you pictures with my paint box?" asked Elisabete.

"Oh, yes! I would love a picture from you," said Paul. "You can send it when Mama writes to me. You make sure she writes to me very often."

Paul set his little sister back on her feet. He stroked her soft curls. Elisabete was the youngest of his seven brothers and sisters. And she was his favorite.

"Do you have your papers?" asked Paul's mother. "Do you have your uncle's letter?"

"Yes, of course he has them," Paul's father replied. "You sewed them into his pocket yourself."

Paul patted his shirt pocket and smiled. "Still there, Mama," he said. "I promise I won't take them out until I arrive in New York."

"Hello-o-o! *Ja*, hello-o-o!" called a loud voice.

The family turned to see a large lady bustling into view. She was overseeing two porters carrying a huge wicker basket.

"Put it there for now," the woman said. "That's right. I'll get someone to carry it on board for me."

The large woman set down her carpet bag. She brushed a wisp of curly red hair from her eyes. Then she smoothed her dark purple dress and adjusted the small matching hat that topped her curls.

"I'm so glad I saw you before we went on board," the lady said to Paul. "I'm sure they'll be boarding us soon. Are you ready?"

"Yes, Frau Borderhoffe," said Paul.

Frau Borderhoffe laughed. "Ah, Paul," she said. "It will be a long trip. You had best call me Harriett."

She gave Paul's mother a long embrace. "Now don't you worry, Greta," Frau Borderhoffe said. "I will watch over your baby duck like he was my own." She looked at his bag and said, "Is that all you brought? Where is your food?"

"The ship is supposed to feed the boy," said Paul's mother, suddenly looking very concerned. "It says so in the paper we signed."

"Yes, if you want him eating gruel and thin soup," said the plump lady. "I was told to bring my own food."

"Oh, George, what will Paul do?" cried his mother, turning to her husband.

"I'll go see what I can find," Paul's father replied. "But I haven't much money left after the ticket." Then he hurried off.

Eight days was a long time to eat gruel. Paul hoped his father would find something.

The crowd that had gathered around them began to move toward the lower gangplank.

"Paul, you can help me get this basket aboard," said Harriett. "Now don't worry, Greta, I won't let your son starve. I have enough here for half the ship!" She laughed loudly, fixing her hat as it tipped over her ear. Her light blue eyes lit up her round face.

Paul gave his mother a tight hug. He didn't dare look into her eyes. He didn't want to cry in front of the others.

Paul's mother hugged him tightly. Then she turned to pick up Elisabete. Paul saw his mother's lips tremble. He took a deep breath and grabbed the wicker handle of the basket. Together Paul and Harriett moved into the stream of people making their way toward the ship.

"Tell Papa to bring whatever he finds to the entrance," Paul said. "I'll wait for him there, after I help Frau Borderhoffe."

"*Auf Wiedersehen!* Good-bye!" called little Elisabete.

"I love you, Mama!" Paul called to his mother as she melted into the crowd.

2

Paul's Chance

"Come on, Paul," said Harriett. "We don't want to get the last bunk near the engine room." She was pulling the basket and Paul with it.

Harriett pushed her way through the crowd. Paul helped her lug the heavy basket up the steep gangplank of the *Kroonland*.

They entered a gaping hole in the ship. He suddenly felt like Jonah, swallowed by a whale. It seemed very dark inside after the bright summer sun.

Soon they reached the ticket taker. A large man in a tight-fitting suit snatched his ticket. He looked at Paul suspiciously.

"Are you traveling alone?" the ticket taker asked.

"Yes, sir," Paul replied. "That is, I'm not going with my family."

"Do you have family in America who will give you work?" questioned the ticket taker.

"Yes, sir," Paul answered quickly. "My uncle and his family have a farm. I am to live with them in Nebraska." He felt uncomfortable under the man's stare.

The ticket taker's dark eyes studied Paul from head to toe. "Very well," he finally said. "You may board."

Harriett handed over her ticket. She gazed down at the little man, folding her arms across her chest. With one quick glance, the ticket taker waved her on board.

Then Paul and Harriett moved farther into the ship. Harriett seemed to know where she wanted to go. So Paul didn't question her many turns.

Many people around them struggled with their

bags. Sometimes the whole line would have to stop and wait while someone ahead adjusted his load.

At last they entered a huge room. Wooden bunks were stacked five layers high. The bunks lined the walls of the room. And there was a row of bunks down the middle. Some of them were wide enough for two people. But many were very narrow.

"This is the men's room," Harriett informed Paul. "You should choose a bunk now. Take a narrow one so you don't have to share with someone who snores." She laughed to herself. "Put your baggage on the bunk. Then sit on it so no one else takes it. I would think it best to be on the top bunk."

Paul climbed up the wooden bunk frame and tossed his bag on the wooden slats of the bed. He tried to ignore the musty smell of the thin, lumpy mattress.

"But I have to go back to meet Papa," said Paul as he climbed back down.

Harriett frowned and then looked around. She spotted a young man with a small boy in tow. She approached the man. "Would you watch this young man's bag while he goes back for something?" asked Harriett.

The man smiled at Paul. "Are you traveling alone?" he asked. Paul shook his head.

"Of course I can help," the man offered. "But don't be too long. I have to go and help my wife in a little while."

"Yes, sir. Thank you," Paul replied. "I will just be a few moments."

"Now go on back," said Harriett. "I'll be able to drag this basket the rest of the way. Through that door is the common room." She pointed at a small door toward the side of the room. "I will meet you on the third-class deck when it's time to sail. Hurry now." She rushed off, dragging her wicker basket.

"Thank you, Harriett," called Paul. "And you too, sir." He tipped his cap and ducked through the long hallway that led back to the entrance.

The entrance was choked with people and baggage. But Paul finally squeezed through to the doorway. He searched for his father but saw no one he knew.

Most of the travelers had already boarded. Only those who remained to wave good-bye to the travelers wandered about on the dock.

Then Paul saw his father running toward him. He was carrying a bundle in his arms. Paul felt very relieved. At least he wouldn't have to eat gruel. His father rushed up to him and pushed a cloth bag into his arms.

After he caught his breath, Paul's father said, "I didn't have much luck, son. There were only a few vendors. But I did see a man selling these dried sausages. He sold me everything he had left."

Paul peeked into the bag to see six huge sausages. He loved sausages!

"Thanks, Papa," Paul said with a grin. "Now everything will be fine. I have my bunk. And a nice man is watching my bag. I'll be fine now."

George Muller looked down at his son. He smiled at Paul and tenderly took him by the shoulders. "I know you will be fine. Write to your mother. This is your chance, Paul. The chance I never got." He pressed Paul to his chest. "I love you, Paul."

"I love you too, Papa," said Paul. Then his father was gone.

Paul stood alone at the entrance of the ship. He turned slowly and made his way back to the men's bunk room, carrying the bulky bag of sausages over his shoulder. The young man and the boy were waiting for him.

"There you are," the man said. "My name is Herr Steiner. This is my son, Markus. Would you watch our bunk while I go and help my wife? She has our little girls."

"Sure," Paul replied as he settled himself on the highest bunk. "I'll be right here until you get back. Do you know when we sail? I was supposed to meet Harriett on deck."

"Not for a while yet," said Herr Steiner. "I'll be back. They'll assign us lockers soon, and then we won't have to worry about our things. You don't snore, do you?" he asked with a laugh.

"Only when I sleep," Paul joked.

The crew boss took Paul's name and recorded his bunk number. Then Paul was given a locker and a key. He locked his bags in his locker.

After Herr Steiner returned, Paul made his way to the deck. It was the first deck above the waterline. Above him, Paul could see the upper decks and the huge pipes of the ship. There were hundreds of third-class passengers. And it seemed to Paul that they were all squeezed onto this deck.

Paul finally found Harriett. She had managed to get them a spot along the railing.

Paul looked out over the port town of Antwerp. He searched the dock for his parents. Finally he caught sight of his sister's shiny yellow curls. There they were! He waved and shouted until he was hoarse.

Mama spotted him and waved back. She showed Elisabete and Paul's father where Paul was standing.

Harriett was waving her handkerchief. *"Auf Wiedersehen! Auf Wiedersehen!"* she shouted.

The deafening sound of the ship's horn drowned all other noise. Paul felt the ship move under him. He knew that he was finally going. He was fifteen years old, and he was sailing to America!

3

On His Way

Paul watched the docks of Antwerp until he could no longer see the people. Slowly, the passengers left the open deck and wandered back to their families. Harriett had told him she must go settle in.

Paul stood at the railing. He watched the town grow smaller and smaller in the distance.

Herr Steiner led Markus up to the railing. He held the small boy in his arms. "See, Son, that is the old world. Today we say good-bye to the Old World. In a few days we will say hello to the New World."

Markus, who was just three, didn't understand. Paul and Herr Steiner laughed.

"I guess he is a bit young," Herr Steiner said. "But today is the most important day of his life. I hope he remembers it."

"I'm sure you will tell him of it many times. He will remember it," Paul assured the man. "My name is Paul Muller." Paul offered his hand.

"Josef Steiner," said the man, shaking Paul's hand. "And you know Markus."

"Pleased to meet you, sir," said Paul. "If you need any more help, please let me know."

"That is very kind of you, Paul," said Herr Steiner. "Where are you going? Do you plan to stay in New York?"

"No," said Paul. "My uncle lives on a farm near a town called Buffalo. It's in Nebraska. My uncle said I can work for him. He says there is still land there. I will go work for him. And I'll save my money to buy some land."

"That's a long trip," said Herr Steiner. "But I hear the prairie is a grand place. We'll be going to Pennsylvania. I'll join someone too. My brother and his family live there. I'm a tailor. We sold everything we had. Our shop, everything . . ." The man stopped speaking and looked out over the wide ocean. "Look, you can't see the land anymore." He sighed.

As the large ship moved farther from the port, the movement of the deck increased. Paul had to hold the railing tightly to keep from falling.

The wind off the water was cold. Paul pulled his jacket close to him. He liked the movement under his feet. He practiced taking a few steps, trying not to lose his balance as the ship tipped and rolled. It seemed that just as he was getting used to the rocking of the ship, it would do something unexpected. This occupied him until nearly sunset.

By then, Paul had mastered the movement. He'd found his way to the forwardmost part of the deck. He hung onto the railing and rode the crests of the waves. And the ship plowed forward, chasing the sinking sun.

Harriett found Paul as he headed for the dinner room. She grabbed him and pushed him in line ahead of her.

"There you are," Harriett said. "I was looking for you in the common room." She smiled as she pretended to scold Paul.

Paul smiled too. "I was on the bow," he said. "It's wonderful on the ship! I love the way she moves!"

"Ah, you are a good sailor," she said.

"I didn't expect to see you here, Harriett," said Paul. "I thought you said the food was awful."

"I hear sometimes it is better, *ja,*" said Harriett. "Some things are good. Eat what is good. Then go back and eat what you bring. That is the best way, *ja?*"

They passed into the dark dining room. Long tables with benches on each side filled the room. A narrow ledge lined the tables.

"The edge is there so the plates won't slide off in bad weather," Harriett said.

Paul wrinkled his nose at the smell of boiled cabbage. It was not his favorite. But he was hungry, so he tried the strange food.

Paul was glad the sausages were locked away for later. He would need them.

"Take a big piece of bread from the basket, Paul," said Harriett. "Pretend you are eating it. The man won't let you take a meal out. But sometimes a piece of bread will slip by."

Late in the evening, Paul pulled out his smuggled piece of bread and a hunk of sausage. He enjoyed a midnight snack.

The next morning, Paul wandered about the ship with little to do. The sleeping area was full of seasick passengers. The common room was filled with small children and chattering women. The men gathered on deck to play cards or dice. They had not asked Paul to join them. Paul had no money to bet even if they had.

So Paul watched the crew going about their work. He noticed one crew member seemed only a bit older than himself. And on the third day at sea, the boy noticed Paul.

"Hello," said the boy. He was rather short but looked older in his blue crew uniform.

"Hello," said Paul. "I'm Paul."

"I'm Hubert," said the boy. "Not much to do, huh? I don't suppose you would like to take a look at the ship sometime, would you?"

"Sure," said Paul. "That would be great!"

"I'll meet you after my shift," said Hubert. "Right here at three o'clock."

"I'll be here," said Paul, excited about a new adventure.

When Hubert and Paul met again, Hubert handed Paul a blue shirt. It was like the one Hubert wore.

"Here," Hubert said. "With this on, no one will question what you are doing. Just follow me and don't talk much if some of the other crew are around."

Paul quickly put on the shirt. "Where are we going?" he asked.

"Well, we can start upstairs with the fancy formal rooms," Hubert replied. "If we are lucky, my uncle will be on duty. Then we can go to the navigation room. Or we could go down to the engine room. Let's just see what happens."

Paul hesitated. "This won't get us into trouble, will it?" he asked.

"No," replied Hubert, laughing. "Just don't go flirting with some pretty girl on A deck."

The boys made their way up the steep stairways to the first-class decks. Paul couldn't believe the beauty of the grand dining room. Soft carpets covered the floor. A huge piano stood in the corner. Although the room was dark, Paul could still see the chandelier gleaming on the ceiling. The room didn't smell like boiled cabbages.

"Nice place," said Hubert. Paul agreed.

Paul loved the navigation room. Hubert's uncle showed them the chart of their voyage. He explained to the boys about shipping lanes and the currents that crossed the North Atlantic.

But Paul thought the engine room was the best of all. Although the noise was deafening, Paul was captivated by the huge turbines that pushed the ship through the water.

Paul watched the engineers move easily around the huge moving pistons. The engineers checked the gauges and turned the valves.

Hubert returned Paul to his deck before dinner. The cool sea breeze felt wonderful after the heat of the engine room. Paul was bubbling over with excitement.

"What a wonderful ship!" Paul exclaimed. "You have such a great job!"

"It's like most jobs," said Hubert with a shrug.

"Well, thanks for the tour," Paul said, shaking hands with Hubert.

"I work late shift tomorrow. But maybe we can do something the next day," said Hubert.

"Aye, aye, captain," saluted Paul.

Paul handed back the borrowed uniform. Then he dashed off to his dinner.

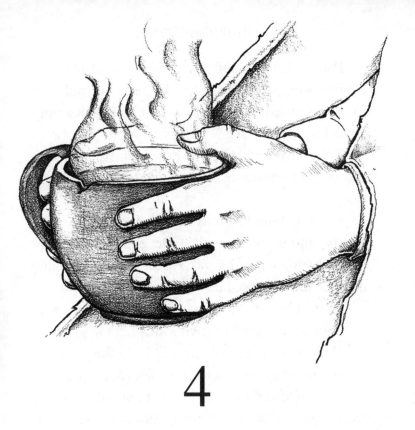

4

Homesick

It rained for the next two days. Paul lay on his bed, staring at the ceiling. Seasick men were moaning in their bunks. And the ship's movement was beginning to bother Paul's stomach.

The common room was filled with families. Every time the ship rolled, things would shift. The women would scream. And the children would cry.

Paul ended up huddled in a corner of the hallway. He was wrapped in a blanket. He felt cold and very lonely. He tried to think of his family. But that only made him feel worse.

This wasn't what he had expected. He looked at his sausage sandwich. But he could hardly take a bite.

Harriett found him asleep in the hallway. She gently shook him awake. He jumped up, not remembering where he was. He knew it must be late because the sky was dark.

"I must have fallen asleep," he said with a yawn.

"Come on, dear," Harriett said. "Let me give you a little soup and tea. No one will be in the common room now. Then we can have a quiet chat."

Paul followed meekly. Harriett poured hot water from a pot on the small stove. Paul held the cup of hot tea between his hands. The tea warmed him. And he slowly woke up.

"We will soon be to America now, *Liebling,*" said Harriett. "Are you doing all right? Do you have enough to eat? Here, try some of this soup. The bread is hard. Dip it in the soup."

Harriett spoke softly to Paul as he did what he was told. Warmth flowed from his center. And soon he felt better. He felt like he was home in his mother's kitchen.

Suddenly, a sharp pang of homesickness struck Paul. It must have shown on his face.

"Tell me about your family," Harriett said. "I have known your mother for years. But I've never had a chance to visit your home. Your mother and I were in school together a long time ago, you know."

"Our farm is outside a small village in south Germany," Paul began. "It's very beautiful there. Our family has been there for many years. Papa always talked about going to America. But Mama never wanted to go. All of our family lives in our village or the one down the road.

"Five years ago, my Uncle Olaf was the first to go to America. Uncle Olaf wrote to us about the beautiful land. He called it 'the prairie.' He asked if I could come to America. And Papa gave me the choice.

"My older brothers will get the farm someday. I could go into a trade, but this seemed better."

Paul shivered, stretched, and then smiled at Harriett. "Thank you for the soup," he said. "I suppose I should go to bed. But Herr Steiner snores so awfully."

"*Ja, ja.* You should hear the noise in the women's room. You would think it was a mining camp," she said, laughing loudly at her joke.

Paul smiled and gave the large woman a big hug. Then he made his way back to his narrow bunk.

———————

The rain continued the following day. Anyone who went on deck was soaked quickly. Paul wanted to stay outside anyway. But he was ordered back inside by a crew member.

"You'll be washed overboard, boy! Go to the common room!" the sailor shouted over the wind.

Hubert found him later that day. But he had extra duty because of the bad weather.

Paul returned to the crowd and stench of the common room. When he arrived, he heard music. Harriett had talked a few of the passengers into singing.

Paul settled into a corner. He listened to an old man singing Russian ballads. Then a young woman sang a funny Irish song. He didn't understand the words, but he caught the meaning. He laughed along with the rest of the audience.

Harriett had talked the crew into brewing strong coffee. And she donated sweet biscuits. Others brought out the last of their supplies to share.

Soon, Paul had tasted the food of several lands. And he offered half of a sausage to the feast. He was really tired of eating sausage anyway. In this way, the day passed quickly.

5

America!

Paul woke early the final morning.

"Paul! Paul!" Herr Steiner called to him. "We will be entering the harbor soon. Get up, boy! You don't want to miss the Statue of Liberty!"

Paul leaped down from his high bunk. He pulled his coat and shoes back on. The morning was damp, but the wind had stopped. He could tell by the gentle way the ship was rocking.

Paul found a place along the railing. As the sun rose, Paul sailed into New York Harbor. The Statue of Liberty welcomed him as she had so many others.

The Statue of Liberty was so much larger than he had imagined. Her torch shone out over the dawn. Many immigrants had gathered on the deck. But they were quiet and still at the sight of the beautiful lady.

Behind the statue, Paul could see New York City. The harbor was full of ships and boats of every size. Small tugboats pushed huge ships into the piers that lined the harbor. He had never seen such tall buildings. Even in the largest city in Germany. It seemed as if New York City stretched forever.

Little tugboats chugged at the ship's sides. Slowly, their ship was guided into the dock. Paul watched from the railing until Harriett shouted to him.

"Paul! Are you not ready, duckling?" Harriett asked. "We need to be some of the first off the ship. Hurry! Hurry, *Liebling!* We want to be at the front of the line. Then we can get through Ellis Island today!" She bustled off to say her good-byes.

Paul returned to the men's bunk room. He

quickly gathered his few belongings. He still had a sausage left.

"Oh, well," Paul thought. "I might get hungry on this island."

He wondered what they had to do there. He asked Harriett as they stood in line to leave the ship.

"The government in America wants to know who is coming into their country," Harriett replied. "They want good, strong people. They will give you tests to see if you can stay."

Paul was terrified. "What kind of tests?" he asked. "What will they do to me? How will I know what to do? How will I understand?"

Harriett patted him on the back. "Don't worry, Paul," she soothed. "You will be just fine. You are a fine, healthy boy. You will not have any problems."

Still, Paul could not relax. They made their way down the gangplank. Several people shouted with joy as they finally touched the ground of America.

The immigrants were taken directly onto a ferry boat. There was only room to stand, but the journey took just a few minutes.

Ellis Island stood before them. It looked to Paul like a huge stone fort. Its stone walls rose four stories high. On each corner was a turret. It reminded Paul of a castle his father had once taken him to see. He wondered if he would make it out again.

As the immigrants landed, they were told in several languages to have their papers ready. And to hold tightly to their bags. Paul carefully undid the button and stitches which held his papers inside his shirt.

As Paul left the ferry, an old man came up to him. The man grabbed Paul's arm and whispered roughly.

"I can get you through all this fast," he told Paul. "Give me your papers. I'll take them to a man I know. He will want a little something for his time. But we can get you through quickly. Do you have some money?"

Paul tried to pull away from the man. But his filthy hand held Paul's arm tightly.

Harriett saw what was happening. She came to Paul's rescue. "Get away! We don't need your help!" she shouted. "Get away!"

Harriett pushed the old man away from Paul. The man slunk off, looking for someone else to prey upon.

Harriett and Paul entered the stone building. Paul gazed at the huge staircase and up to the second floor. He could see people peering down from over the railing. The new immigrants picked up their belongings and began the steep climb.

Paul realized that Harriett no longer had her large wicker basket.

"Harriett, where is your basket?" Paul asked. "Did you forget it?"

Harriett laughed and patted her ample tummy. "We ate everything in it, so I left it behind," she answered. "I only have my few clothes to carry now. Don't worry about me, *Liebling*. I can make it."

As they headed up the steps, Paul tried to show the inspectors above how easy it was for him. But by the time he reached the top, his back ached from carrying his bag.

A few people had dropped back, unable to make the climb. Relatives were told not to help each other. Each person was expected to make the climb on his own.

At the top, men were led one way and women another way. Harriett gave him a big smile as they parted ways.

Paul was taken into a large room with many other men. He had seen a few of them on board the ship. He was asked to prove his name and birth date.

A gruff old man with thick glasses spoke to him first. "Where are you bound? Who will give you a job?" He looked over Paul's papers and the letter from his uncle.

Paul must have answered the man's questions correctly because he kept moving down the line. He was very tired of standing in line. But everyone waited patiently, leaning quietly against the metal bars.

A young doctor examined him. The doctor looked carefully at his eyes and listened to his chest.

"Don't be scared. I won't hurt you," said the doctor in German.

"You speak German?" asked Paul.

"Only a few words," responded the doctor. He smiled at Paul. "You are fine."

The doctor said he was fit. Paul was given the papers he would need. Then he was taken back onto the ferryboat.

Harriett waved to Paul as she, too, boarded the ferry.

"Now that wasn't too difficult, *ja?*" Harriett said wiping her forehead with a handkerchief. She puffed for a moment. Then she sat down heavily next to Paul on the wooden bench. It was a warm afternoon, with little breeze to stir the air.

"Do you have your train ticket?" Harriett asked. "Do you know how to get to the station?"

"I have the ticket," Paul said. "Papa had it sent before I left Germany. One of the last men I spoke to said there is a trolley. He gave me the number. He told me the correct money to have." Paul opened his palm to show three small copper coins. "I will have to wait at the station for the train. But I will be fine. Where do you go now, Harriett?"

"Ah, my sister Gretchen will be waiting for me when the ferryboat lands," said Harriett. "She knew the day I was to arrive. She will be there."

"And will you live with her?" asked Paul.

"*Ja,* I will," said Harriett. "I will help in her store, and we will live above it. Her husband died last year, poor thing! She asked me to come."

The ferry's motor rumbled to life, and Paul could see the crew preparing to cast off.

"Do you know if the Steiners are done on the island?" asked Paul. "I don't see them on the ferry." He searched the crowd for his friend.

"Ah, I think there is trouble for them. Their little girl has problems with her eyes. I saw them going off to the hospital area," Harriett replied, shaking her head. "They may be there for a while. They cannot leave such a little one behind."

As the ferry pulled away from the pier, Paul stared over the side at the fortress called Ellis Island. He felt lucky to be continuing his journey.

After a quick, bumpy ride across the harbor, they

had truly landed in New York City. Before they left the boat, Harriett gave Paul a smothering hug.

"It has been good to know you, Paul," Harriett said. "Will you write to me? Here is my address. Do you have everything tucked back in that pocket of yours?"

"Yes, ma'am," replied Paul. "Thank you for all of your help."

Harriett smiled down at him. "You will make your mama and papa proud," she said. "Here, I have a little something for you."

Paul looked down at the small book she held in her hand. It said "English" on the dark red cover.

Paul smiled. "Thank you," he said.

Just ahead, Paul could see a woman who looked exactly like Harriett. The woman was even dressed in purple. As the woman caught sight of Harriett, she began to scream and wave her hands in the air.

"Hitty! Hitty!" the other woman cried.

Harriett saw her sister. The two hugged with tears and a great deal of noise. Harriett's purple hat fell off her head.

Paul watched the happy reunion. Then he turned to search for the number eight trolley to Grand Central Station.

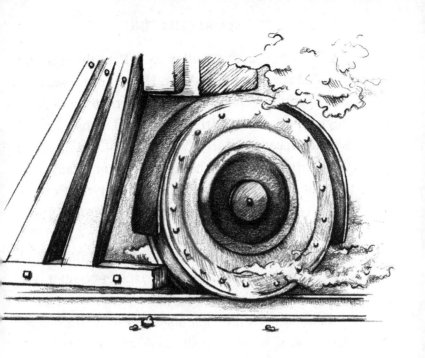

6

The Train Ride

Paul climbed the steps of the trolley. He realized that he was truly on his own.

Around him, people spoke many languages. But he did not understand. A moment of panic overtook him. Then he felt for the gift that Frau Borderhoffe had given him. He would start to learn English tonight.

The horse-drawn trolley took Paul through the crowded streets of New York. He had never seen so many people. Vendors shouted. Carriages and carts clogged the streets. Brightly colored signs adorned every surface.

Finally, they reached the station. Paul had thought Ellis Island was big. But Grand Central Station was enormous. From here, the grand trains of America reached out across the vast land.

After a long walk through the huge building and much searching, Paul found the ticket counter. He asked for the train to Nebraska.

Paul showed the man his ticket to Buffalo. The clerk looked at him and shrugged his shoulders, not understanding. Luckily, the clerk next to him heard Paul's question in German and interrupted.

"Sprechen Sie Deutsch?" he asked Paul.

"Ja!" said Paul. Paul asked where he could find the train he needed. He learned it would leave at eight o'clock that evening from track six.

"Danke," said Paul

"I must begin my English now," he thought to himself. He had two hours to wait for the train. He ate some of his sausage, sat on a hard wooden bench, and studied his English book.

By the time he boarded the train, Paul could

speak some English. "My name is Paul Muller. I am going to Nebraska."

———————————————

The movement of the train and the clack of its steel wheels made Paul sleepy. Sitting upright in third class, he leaned his head against his bag and slept. The conductor only bothered him once to check his ticket.

Paul awoke hungry the next morning. He decided he would buy himself some food at the next stop.

Paul settled down to watch the green rolling hills of eastern Pennsylvania. He studied his English. He learned how to ask for bread, fruit, water, and cheese.

Paul carefully pulled some money from his sock. He made sure no one saw him. Except for trolley fare, he hadn't touched the money at all.

As the train pulled into a small town station, Paul made his way to the exit. He didn't dare leave his things on board. So he lugged them with him.

Soon Paul saw the vendors. They came to sell their things to the daily passengers on the westbound train.

Paul chose fresh apples, a loaf of bread, cheese, and some little fruit pies. He hadn't had a fruit tart since his Mama had baked one for his going away. He thought of her as he climbed back aboard the train.

The day passed quickly. He found a nice old German man to talk to for a bit of the way.

They chugged slowly through the mountains. Sometimes the train entered black tunnels or crossed tall trestle bridges. There were a few more stops, but Paul stayed in his seat.

The conductor had told him he would have to change trains in Lincoln, Nebraska. But that was not for a few days. So Paul studied his small English book again.

Paul found English pretty easy because so many of his words were similar. He practiced over and over again. "How do you do? My name is Paul Muller. I come from Germany. I am looking for my Uncle Olaf."

Finally he could do it without looking at the book. He felt very pleased as he drifted off to sleep.

In the night, Paul felt a hand moving his bag out from under him. Sleep made him slow to react. But then, suddenly, he was wide awake.

A man stood over him, his hands on Paul's bag.

Paul shouted, "No, thief! No! That's mine!" He held firmly to his bag.

The thief shoved Paul back against the seat. Then he made a grab for Paul's bag. Stunned, Paul held on tightly.

"No, no!" Paul shouted.

Then the conductor had ahold of the man. And another passenger helped to hold the thief.

"He tried to steal my things," Paul shouted in German.

"I don't understand," said the conductor. But he held on to the struggling man.

Paul grabbed his English book and quickly looked up the word he wanted. He pointed to the man and said, "Thief."

"That's what I thought," said the conductor. "Caught you, finally. You come with me now." He pushed the thief ahead of him. "Good job, sonny," the conductor called over his shoulder.

Paul sat down, completely out of breath. He was shaking. There was no more sleep for him. He held tightly to his bag the rest of the night.

The train crept across the land. It went through smoke-filled cities and wide countrysides.

Another day passed slowly. Paul's back ached from the hard seat. At one stop, he got off the train and ran around the station three times just to stretch his legs.

Paul noticed the next morning that the rolling hills had flattened out in the night. The train now dashed west across the flat and treeless land. It seemed to stretch forever in the distance.

The towns were much farther apart now. And they were smaller than they had been yesterday.

When Paul arrived in Lincoln the following afternoon, he was tired. But he wanted to continue his journey. He hoped Uncle Olaf would have a big meal and a warm bed ready when he arrived.

Paul was disappointed when he learned he had a long wait in Lincoln. He decided to treat himself to dinner in the cafe next to the station. He felt he deserved warm food. And besides, the conductor had given him a shiny half-dollar for helping catch the thief.

When he entered the cafe, he wondered how he would order his meal. He only knew a few words in English. But the waitress, a smiling round woman, soon recognized his accent. She began speaking to Paul in German.

"Where are you from?" she asked. "How long have you been in America? It is so good to speak to someone from the old country."

She brought him a wonderful meal, and they had a long chat.

Paul slept on the wooden bench in the station. The train to Buffalo would not be along until the following morning. He tied his bag tightly to his hand and slept on top of it. No one would catch him unaware again.

───────────

The following morning, Paul was excited as he boarded the small train. He was on the last part of his journey. He had managed to travel halfway around the world, all by himself. And he was just fifteen years old.

Paul decided he would write to his mother that evening. He would tell her all about his journey.

He watched the wide prairie pass slowly by. There were times he couldn't spot a single tree across the land. The grass was green, but most of the fields were golden.

Sometimes he saw a small house or a traveler on a dusty road. Paul couldn't believe the size of Nebraska.

Finally, the old conductor called, "Buffalo! Buffalo!"

Paul jumped from his seat and waited at the door. He knew that no one would be there to meet him. After all, they didn't know exactly when he was coming.

But still, deep inside, he hoped someone would be there.

7

Prairie Meeting

As the train pulled away, Paul looked out over his new town. Its one wide, dusty street had only a few buildings. There were a few shacks scattered at the town's edges.

Paul knew that the train tracks had just reached Buffalo. The station had a small platform and a tiny shack used to sell tickets. Two trains each week came through Buffalo.

Paul looked around for someone to show him the way to his Uncle Olaf's. He saw a boy about his own age walking up the street. The boy carried a large feed sack on his back.

Paul stepped toward the boy. "Hello," he said in his carefully practiced English. "My name is Paul Muller. I am from Germany. I am looking for my Uncle Olaf."

"Excuse me?" said the boy. He couldn't understand Paul. The boy set down the heavy sack.

Paul tried again. This time more slowly. But the boy still looked confused.

"Olaf Muller?" Paul repeated. "Olaf Muller?"

"Oh," said the boy. "My name is Roy. Roy." Roy pointed to himself as he said his name. "Come." He pulled gently on Paul's arm.

Paul smiled and picked up his bag. He hoped the boy understood.

The boy took Paul down the street to one of the large buildings. Above the door, a sign said "Henneman's General Store."

As Paul and the boy entered, the boy called out.

"This boy, I think he is German. He is asking for Olaf Muller. I can't understand him very well."

Roy's father was standing at the counter talking with Mr. Henneman.

Mr. Henneman stepped forward. "Hello, Roy," he said to the boy. Then he turned to Paul. *"Sprechen Sie Deutsch?"*

"Ja," said Paul. Then he continued in German. "I am looking for Olaf Muller. I am his nephew. He asked me to come from Germany to live with him. Can you help me find him?"

"What did he say?" asked Roy.

"Well, he says he's Olaf's nephew, and he's looking for him," Mr. Henneman said. "What will the poor boy do? Olaf sent a letter back to Germany three months ago. Olaf knew he was pulling out. He was telling his brother not to send the boy."

"I wonder if the letter ever got there," said Roy. "Poor guy. What's he going to do? Does anyone know where Olaf went?"

"No," replied Mr. Henneman. "After his wife died, he sold his place and took off with his two boys."

Roy looked at his dad. "There's room in the old house," he said. "Or he could sleep in the barn. You said yourself you wished we had an extra pair of hands."

"I don't know, Roy," said Roy's father. "We don't know the boy. And we can't even talk to him. How will I tell him what to do?"

"Don't worry, Dad," said Roy. "I'll help. I'll bet he catches on quickly. He came all this way. We can't let him starve."

John Arnold sighed. "Tell him, Henneman."

Mr. Henneman told the news to Paul in German. At first Paul was very upset. But it seemed that the boy and his father were trying to help. He realized he had nowhere else to go.

He climbed aboard their wooden wagon for the ride across the prairie.

"Home, Molly," John said, clicking to the old horse.

Paul rode in the back of the bumpy wooden wagon. The land was the flattest land he'd ever seen. There were no hills or trees. The cloudless, deep blue sky seemed like a huge overturned bowl.

Roy smiled at Paul. Roy chatted and pointed to things. Paul knew that the boy was trying to teach him the English words for the things around him.

"Horse," said Roy.

Paul repeated after Roy. "Horse."

"Wagon," Roy said.

Paul repeated again. "Vagon."

By the time they arrived at the homestead, Paul could say, "I ride the horse, and I drive the vagon."

Roy jumped down from the wagon as they neared the front door of a small wooden house. He called, "Fern, Fern! You'll never believe who we found in town."

A half-grown girl with long blonde braids walked out of the house. She had a baby on her hip.

"Stop shouting, Roy," the girl said. "You'll scare Johnny to death!"

Fern handed the baby to her mother. Then she stepped forward to meet the boy in strange clothing.

Paul jumped down from the wagon.

"Paul," Roy said, "this is my sister Fern. Fern." He repeated her name so Paul would understand.

Paul grinned at the girl, repeating her name. "Fern." He took off his hat and made a low sweeping bow before her. He did the same before Roy's mother. Fern giggled and curtsied to him.

Roy explained Paul's problem to his mother and sister.

"Poor boy," Ma said. "What can we do to get in touch with Olaf? Does anyone know where he is?"

"Henneman said he would send out a few wires to the towns farther west," said Roy's dad. "We might find him. Until then, there wasn't much else we could do."

"Roy, I think this is the biggest thing you've ever drug home to care for," said Fern, laughing.

"Well, he doesn't need a cage. But I'll bet he needs feeding," said Ma. "Fern, you go get a few more vegetables from the garden. Roy, you go and get some water heated so our guest can get cleaned up. I guess he'll have to sleep in the barn loft tonight."

"Maybe later he can sleep in the old sod house," suggested Roy.

"Perhaps," said Ma.

As the family sat down to dinner that evening, Paul took out his English book.

"Thank you," he said. "You are good friends."

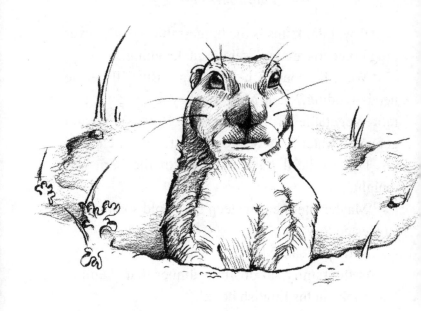

8

Paul Meets Peeker

After breakfast, Ma asked Fern to clean out the little sod house for Paul. Fern had hoped to visit a friend. But she sighed and didn't complain.

Fern tried not to burden her mother too much. Since the baby had been born, Ma had even more to do. Fern tried to help, but it seemed that Ma always looked very tired.

Fern gazed at her mother, Marie. She was still pretty. But the years on the prairie had left her thin. Her face had tiny lines.

They had moved from the sod house early last summer. It had taken Dad almost a year to build the new house. He worked on it in the evenings and whenever the other farm work was done.

Roy and Fern had both hammered until their arms ached. They wanted to get it finished before the baby came.

They had just finished the house when Johnny was born. Now the sod house was used for storage.

Fern walked to the sod house with cleaning rags, a broom, and a bucket. Paul wanted to help her, but she tried to shoo him away. He kept saying, "I help. I help."

Fern finally gave him the broom just to quiet him. She had to admit he did a good job.

While they worked, Paul chatted to Fern in German. Although she didn't understand his words, his voice was soft. He smiled all the time.

When they had finished, the two-room sod house looked very homey. The old, handmade table and chairs stood near a tiny window. A small bed was moved into the corner where Fern's parents used to sleep. The old "hot belly" stove was still there, but Paul wouldn't need that in the summer.

"Good," said Paul, looking around at his new home.

"I'll have to show Paul our friend Peeker," Roy said at dinner.

"I don't suppose they have prairie dogs in Germany," said Dad.

"Have you seen his mate lately?" Fern asked. "Pop is so cute, but she sure is shy."

"Pop just hasn't gotten to know us yet. She'll come around," Roy assured his sister.

Roy had rescued the injured Peeker. And the little prairie dog had chosen to live near the Arnolds' home after he got well.

After two years with the Arnolds, he had suddenly disappeared one spring. He returned a few weeks later with a shy little female.

Roy turned to Paul. "Do you know 'prairie dog'? 'Prairie dog'?" he asked Paul. Roy did an imitation of Peeker, holding his hands under his chin and wiggling his nose.

Paul copied Roy. "Prairie dog," Paul said, wiggling his nose.

Fern burst out laughing.

"Fern!" scolded her mother. But Ma was having a hard time keeping a straight face too.

"Prairie dog!" Paul said again with one more nose wiggle.

After dinner, Roy took Paul to see the little animals. Peeker had built his den near the old sod house. He'd stayed there even after the Arnold family had moved into the new house.

Roy made a special whistling noise. The small, furry animal peeked his head out of his den. Peeker's bright eyes sparkled. His little nose never stopped moving.

Roy placed a handful of dried corn in Paul's hand. Then Paul sat down on the ground.

Peeker smelled his favorite treat. He moved slowly toward Paul's outstretched hand. But the smell of the corn won out.

Peeker put his paws on Paul's lap and feasted on the corn. After a while, Peeker even let Paul stroke the soft brown fur of his back.

Halfway through the meal, Peeker gave a shrill whistle. The boys could hear a returning call from below the ground. But instead of peering out, the little female suddenly *popped* out of the ground. She gave a piercing whistle. Paul jumped.

"That's why we call her Pop," laughed Roy.

"Yes, I see. Pop!" laughed Paul.

Paul put a little corn on the ground near her. Pop scolded Paul as he moved closer to her. But she accepted the corn as Paul backed up.

The two animals chattered at the boys. Then they darted back into their den.

"Prairie dog," Roy said.

"*Ja,* prairie dog," repeated Paul.

As the boys returned to the house, Roy announced, "Peeker likes Paul! Even Pop came out for a visit."

Fern frowned a bit. She said to herself, "*Everyone* likes Paul."

After Paul said goodnight, he returned to the small sod house. It was very cool inside the thick dirt walls, even though the evening was warm.

Paul sat at the table for a long time. He thought about all the things that had happened to him. It had been less than a month ago that he'd lived in Germany with his family.

He wanted to write to his mother. He'd promised that he would. The paper, pen, and ink waited on the table where Mrs. Arnold had left it.

He lit the oil lamp and began.

Dear Mama,

I am doing very well in Buffalo. You may have gotten Uncle Olaf's letter by now. He has moved away from Buffalo.

I am working for a very nice family. They

have a boy almost my age and very pretty girl. I work hard for them so they will want me to stay.

We are trying to find Uncle Olaf, but I don't know what I will do even if we do. I think of you often, and I miss you.

Give my little Itty a hug and a kiss. Please write to me soon. I enjoyed the voyage. New York is even bigger than Uncle Olaf said!

Your son, Paul

9
Fern Gets Jealous

After chores the next afternoon, Roy asked Paul if he would like to go fishing. Roy acted out the activity. Then Paul understood.

Roy repeated the word, "Fishing. Fishing." Finally, Paul could say it too.

The two boys went off laughing and shouting, "Fishing!"

Fern watched as the boys headed for the creek. She couldn't hide the frown on her face as her mother watched her.

Fern shrugged and went to play with Johnny. The baby cooed at her and giggled when she tickled his fat tummy. He lay in the cradle that their dad had carved for him last winter.

"Sometimes it's hard to share your special people with others," Ma said. She was stirring the pot on the big iron stove.

Fern shrugged again. "Roy usually asks me to go fishing," she said. "I'm a good fisherman." The hurt poured out. "I don't know if I like Paul."

"Sometimes feelings can get very mixed up when you're young," said Ma. "It's hard to tell what you feel. Just be kind."

Fern remembered back to when Johnny had first been born. She'd felt angry at the poor little thing, not understanding why. Somehow, this felt the same. Ma had called it *jealousy*. Fern wished it would go away.

The boys came home with a string of fish, enough for dinner. Paul cleaned them, and Ma fried them in cornmeal.

"Well, at least you make yourself useful, Paul," said Dad, finishing off a second helping.

Although Paul didn't understand the words, he knew he was appreciated.

Paul worked hard every day. He had taken over milking the cow. Every morning he cleaned out Molly's stall. He weeded the vegetable garden and helped with hoeing in the fields. He was exhausted by dark. But he took time each day to study his English book.

Roy was very helpful, carefully explaining and showing Paul what to do. Many of the chores were the same as those Paul had done on his parents' farm. And he was used to hard work.

Fern was still quiet around him. Sometimes Paul would try to say something to her in English. He would forget the words or change them all around. He felt so foolish.

Paul sat down one evening on the front porch with Fern.

"May I sit?" he said in English.

"Yes, of course," Fern replied.

"It is pretty night, *ja?*" Paul continued.

"Yes," said Fern. She didn't know what to say. She finally jumped up and said, "I need to go check on Johnny." She didn't really, but it was the only thing she could think of. She hurried away.

Paul sighed and looked up at the stars. "Poor frightened little deer," he said in German. "Someday, I vill not frighten you so."

From the window of her darkened room, Fern watched Paul on the front porch. She decided that she would just ignore him.

10

The Outing

The Arnold family and Paul piled into the wagon one warm Saturday afternoon. They were going into Buffalo for an outing.

Ma had several pies, a ham, and some fresh bread in a basket. There was a picnic and dance in town that night. People from miles around would be gathering for the fun.

Paul had brushed his suit and shoes so he looked his best. The whole family was looking forward to the party.

First, Dad needed to collect some supplies at Henneman's.

As they entered the general store, Mr. Henneman greeted Paul in German. "Hello, Paul," said Mr. Henneman. "How are you?"

"Very well, sir," Paul said. "It is very nice to speak German to someone. Sometimes my head hurts from trying to remember the English words."

Mr. Henneman laughed. "I know," he said. "It took almost a year before I could think in English. Then it got much easier. You are doing very well, I hear. I have something for you."

Paul saw the small letter in Mr. Henneman's hand. He recognized the handwriting on the envelope.

A letter from home! "Thank you, sir!" Paul exclaimed. "It's from home!"

"What is it, Paul?" Roy asked. He noticed how excited his friend was.

"It's a letter from my family!" Paul said in English.

"Don't just stand there looking at it," said Roy. "Read it!"

Paul carefully opened the fragile envelope and began reading.

My dearest Paul,

We got your Uncle Olaf's letter two weeks after you had sailed. We were very worried for you. We are glad that you have found such a good family. Bless them for their warm hearts.

Itty misses you very much. She has painted many pictures for you. It was very hard to choose the one she most wanted to send.

We think of you every day and hope your new life is safe and happy. Summer had her puppies—six in all! Daisy had twin foals. Itty wanted to name one of the foals after you.

Take care of yourself. Papa sends his love.

Mama

Paul carefully unfolded the painting made by his sister so far away. It was a picture of him standing next to two baby horses.

Paul was glad that the Arnold family had left him alone while he read his letter. He brushed the tears away. Then he rejoined them in the wagon.

"Everything is fine," Paul said. "I have a horse named after me." He tried to smile.

Ma gave him a quick hug. And he felt a little better.

The party was held in front of the school. Makeshift tables were lined up under the trees. They were weighted down with the feast everyone had made.

Roy introduced Paul to some of the young people. A few spoke German in their homes, so Paul felt welcome.

The music started after dinner. Paul stood on the side, watching couples dancing. He tried to understand the group dance where people were trading partners.

"It's called a square dance," Roy said, walking toward Paul. "It's really not that hard. You just follow what everyone else is doing. You should give it a try."

"Vould I need a partner?" asked Paul.

"Yes," Roy said. "Go ask Fern. Go on! She loves to dance!"

Roy pushed Paul over to where Fern was standing. She saw them coming. But she was very surprised when Roy said, "Come on, Fern. Paul wants to square dance."

Before either could object, Paul and Fern were joining the whirling dancers. Paul quickly caught the rhythm. And by the second pass, he could follow the steps.

Paul and Fern whirled to the fiddle player and laughed together. As the music stopped, they were hand in hand. Paul took off his cap and bowed low before Fern. She looked very pretty. Her cheeks were flushed and her eyes were smiling.

"Thank you, fair lady," Paul said.

Fern blushed and was gone.

11

Paul's Decision

Paul stayed on through the harvest. Dad said it was a good thing he had come or they never would have finished before the rains.

Paul worked hard in the fields all day. Then he helped with the dishes after dinner. There were so many more dishes to wash with all the extra hands who came to help.

Paul was good with the horses. It took eight horses to pull the huge combine. So Paul often drove the machine in measured rows across the fields.

The farm had grown bigger in the last few years. Pa had been able to buy land from other farmers who did not want to stay on. It took many men to bring in the corn.

At dinner, the crew and family ate outside under the willow tree. The long tables were filled with food. Fresh bread, fresh baked pies, stew, and vegetables covered the table. Fern and her mother worked from before light until long after dark in the hot kitchen.

On the last day of the harvest, Paul came in early and watched as Fern finished peeling apples. She carefully turned the apple so that the entire skin was removed in a long coil.

"You do that good," Paul said. "My mama can do that too. Ven she makes strudel." Fern smiled as Paul walked out the kitchen door.

There had been no word from Uncle Olaf all summer.

Then in late fall, a letter arrived. Dad brought the letter home from town one Saturday.

Olaf was in Montana. He'd heard Paul had arrived in Buffalo. He sent a letter asking Paul to come north before winter.

Paul read the letter and tried to sort out his feelings. He wanted very much to see his uncle again. And yet he had found a good family here. He wanted to stay with them.

Paul spoke to Roy that afternoon.

"I feel very sad to leave Buffalo," Paul said. "Your family has been good to me. I don't vant to go."

"Well, I'll miss you," Roy said. "And I know my folks will. You've been a big help this harvest. But I'll bet Fern will miss you the most." Roy smiled and gave Paul a nudge in the ribs.

"Do you think so?" Paul asked. "She von't speak to me. I don't think she likes me."

"She likes you," Roy said. "I know it. She just needs some time to grow up. She's just thirteen."

Paul thought about it. "I think I vill go see my uncle," he decided. "But in a vile, I vill come back. Ven ve are both older."

Paul announced his decision at dinner.

"I was going to put up some credit for you at Henneman's," Dad said. "But now you'll need the money you earned this season instead. We'll go into town tomorrow and get it. You did a man's work, so you will be paid for it."

"Thank you," Paul said. "There should be enough to pay for my ticket. Uncle Olaf sent some money too. You have all been so kind. I hope to come see you again someday." Paul looked at Fern as he spoke.

Fern looked at the table and did not reply.

12
Paul's Promise

Dad took Paul into town the next afternoon. They visited the bank and then bought Paul's train ticket.

Paul would leave the following Saturday. He'd have to change trains several times on the way to Montana. But Paul wasn't worried. He'd grown several inches taller in the last months. He could speak and understand English. He knew he could fend for himself.

As the two rode home, Dad said, "We'll all miss you, Paul. But I guess Fern will miss you the most."

Paul stared at his shoes. "I'll miss her too, sir," he said. "I have strong feelings for her, you know."

"Yes, I guessed as much," said Dad. "I think you're a very wise young man. Fern needs a bit more growing up. We do hope you come back someday."

"Yes, sir. I vill, sir," Paul said with a smile.

———————

Ma looked over Paul's clothes carefully. "I think I can alter these very easily," she said. "Your mother left plenty of room for you to grow."

Ma measured Paul's arms and shoulders with her measuring tape. "I'll have your coat finished in a day or two. Then we can lengthen the trousers," she continued. "You'll need a rough coat for the winter. I hope your uncle can find you something."

"He and my two cousins may have something I can use," Paul said. "Or I vill earn it. In his letter, Uncle Olaf said more men are needed for the vinter on the ranch. He has a job for me. I'll be just fine."

"Only two more days," said Ma.

"Only two more days," Paul repeated, a little sadly.

━━━━━━━━━━

That evening, Paul again asked if he might sit with Fern on the front porch. It had been very warm the last few evenings. Roy had called it an "Indian summer."

Fern again did not know what to say to the boy who had joined their family. She was about to run away. But Paul spoke.

"Please sit with me for a minute, Fern," he said. "I vould like to talk vith you. It is very hard to find the right English words ven you are always running avay."

Fern smiled at him and sat back down. "I'm sorry, Paul. You've done very well learning English. You can say almost anything you vish to now," she giggled.

Paul laughed. He knew that he could never get the 'v' and 'w' correct.

"I'm very fond of you, Fern," Paul said. "I have special feelings for you. You and I are too young to understand these feelings. But someday I vish to come see you again."

"I know," Fern said with a sigh. "I guess that's why I run away. I'll miss you." She stood up to go. Then she said, "Wait a moment. I'll be right back."

Fern disappeared through the door and into the house. In a moment she returned carrying a small book.

"I found this a month ago at Henneman's," Fern said. "I bought it for you." Fern held the small blue book out for him to take. It said "English Poetry" on the cover.

Paul stood and took the book from her. He gently touched the blonde braids that hung past her shoulders. "Ven these are gone," he said, "I vill return."